I0757484

This book belongs to:

Khaldoun and The Cape of Wonder

Written by Jessica Koenig

Illustrated by Jessica Koenig & Ismail Mustafa

Brooklyn, New York

ISBN: 979-8-9990336-6-6
LCCN: 2025922655

For Khaldoun —

*May you always see the magic in the world,
and the bravery that's already inside you.*

In a city of sunshine and buildings so high,
Lived little Khaldoun with dreams of flying in the sky.

With curls that bounced and sneakers so bright,
Khaldoun dreamed of flying when tucked in at night.

Each morning he'd stand by the mirror and say,
"I'm brave, I'm kind, I'll do good today."

He dashed through the mall with a laugh and a spin,
His cape caught the breeze as his quests would begin!

POW!

His cape wasn't magic. Not stitched with gold thread,
but sewn from his dreams and the books that he read.

One stormy day, with thunderous sound,
A shadow appeared that shook the whole ground!

A monster came stomping, it roared with a sneer,
People cried out, "KHALDOUN, STEER CLEAR".

But heroes don't hide when the world needs their spark,
Khaldoun stood tall and lit up the dark.

Khaldoun darted through alleys, so narrow and tight,
His cape caught the wind and shimmered with light.

Khaldoun leapt on a bench, then bounced off a wall,
"This monster," he shouted, "doesn't scare me at all!"

Khaldoun whistled and waved with a bright glowing light,
"Hey monster! Come chase me, let's see if you bite!"

TOYS
STYLE

The beast gave a growl and quickened his pace,
But Khaldoun sped forward, ready to race!

He zipped through the fountain, dashed over a wall,
Khaldoun raced forward, not frightened at all!

With one final jump, he reached a tall gate,
Behind it, the monster would soon meet its fate.

Khaldoun opened his pouch and tossed out magic sand,
Magic from books now alive in his hand!

The monster huffed loudly and slumped to the ground,
His big glowing eyes stared sadly around.
He'd tried to be scary, but now felt so small,
His roar didn't matter that much after all.

It sniffled and whimpered, "I'm lost and alone...
I didn't mean to frighten you, I just want a home!"

Khaldoun stood still, then lowered his guard,
A hero shows empathy, even when it is hard.

He offered his hand and said, "Come with me.
Let's find you a place where you're safe as can be."

They walked through the city, side by side,
The people amazed and staring wide-eyed.

The Sheikh came out and declared with a cheer,
"Our city is safe with the young hero here!"

The monster found work planting flowers in rows,
Digging in dirt using hands, teeth, and toes!

And Khaldoun loves to fly just mostly pretend,
But every adventure he finds kindness to extend.

He doesn't need lasers or muscles of steel,
Just courage to help and a heart that can heal.

So if you see shadows or tremble at night,
Think like Khaldoun, be brave, smart, and bright!
Because heroes aren't only found in a cape,
They live in your heart, and come in every shape.
With love from your family lighting your way,
You'll find all the courage to face each day.

You can be
a hero too!

And next time you leap with a shout or a cheer...
Remember: a hero like YOU lives right here.

www.ingramcontent.com/pod-product-compliance
Lightning Source LLC
Chambersburg PA
CBHW040746010826
48981CB00035B/335